John Hunter

Observations and Reflections on Geology

SALZWASSER
VERLAG

John Hunter

Observations and Reflections on Geology

Reprint of the original, first published in 1859.

1st Edition 2022 | ISBN: 978-3-37513-322-1

Verlag (Publisher): Salzwasser Verlag GmbH, Zeilweg 44, 60439 Frankfurt, Deutschland
Vertretungsberechtigt (Authorized to represent): E. Roepke, Zeilweg 44, 60439 Frankfurt, Deutschland
Druck (Print): Books on Demand GmbH, In de Tarpen 42, 22848 Norderstedt, Deutschland

OBSERVATIONS AND REFLECTIONS

ON

GEOLOGY

BY

JOHN HUNTER, F.R.S.

INTENDED TO SERVE AS

AN INTRODUCTION TO THE CATALOGUE

OF HIS

COLLECTION OF EXTRANEOUS FOSSILS.

LONDON:
PRINTED BY TAYLOR AND FRANCIS,
RED LION COURT, FLEET STREET.

1859.

PREFACE.

THE Introduction mentioned in the title-page is contained in two Hunterian Manuscripts, now in the possession of the Royal College of Surgeons of England. The first of these, a thin quarto of seventy-two pages, bound in calf, and lettered on the back, is in the handwritings of two of Mr. Hunter's well-known assistants and amanuenses, Messrs. W. Bell and W. Clift. It is marked "PART THE FIRST." The second Manuscript, entirely in Mr. Clift's handwriting, contains an accurate copy from the first Manuscript, of PART FIRST, with a continuation and conclusion of the subject, entitled PART SECOND. It is believed that this Second Part must have been copied by Mr. Clift from an original MS. (probably furnished by Capt. Sir E. Home), nothing being known of such original among the papers of the College.

The manner in which the original MS., PART FIRST, came into the possession of the College, is fully explained by the following memorandum, in the handwriting of Mr. Clift, prefixed to the contents of the second Manuscript.

" On the day of the delivery of the Hunterian Oration, Feb. 14, 1839, at the entrance into the Theatre of the Visitors and Council, Mr. Keate put into my hands a thin volume, desiring me to look at it *afterwards.* Mr. Keate had doubtless (or probably) just received it from Captain Sir Everard Home, who was among the Visitors. This volume had evidently been lately bound in calf, and contains a portion of Mr. Hunter's Manuscript Introduction to a History of Fossils, and consists of seventy-two leaves written on one side, and numerous additions on the opposite or blank pages. It is evidently *only a part* of the MS., by the catchword at the foot of the *last* page.

" The Bookbinder had been directed to put on the back—

" ' HUNTER's CATALOGUE (! !) OF FOSSILS,' and within, on the title-page, in Capt. Home's handwriting, ' CATALOGUE OF MR. HUNTER's *Cabinet of Fossils now in the Col. of Surgeons, corrected by himself.*'

" N.B. That this manuscript was one of those which Mr. Hunter revised and made many additions to, in *probably* the *last year* of his life, but *certainly* within the *last two,* is evident from the fact that many of the pages are in my handwriting, and occasionally afterwards interlined and amended by additions in Mr. Hunter's handwriting ; and some of the additional notes are begun by Mr. Hunter, and were then given to me to copy-in the remainder of the sentence from his loose slips.

" This volume is certainly a curiosity in its way ; and *after this,* one need not despair of seeing the fabulous Phœnix proved to be *no fable,* and both him and the Dodo emerge from their *ashes* or their other obscure haunts.

" WILLIAM CLIFT."

Mr. Clift not having received any communication, either in writing or verbally, from Mr. Keate concerning the Volume described over leaf, wrote the following Note to Mr. Keate, desiring further instructions concerning its disposal :—

" Museum, Royal College of Surgeons,
March 14, 1839.

" SIR,

" Will you be so good as to inform me whether the Volume which you put into my hands, on the day of the last Oration, be intended as a present to the College or Museum, or a loan similar to the other papers which Captain Sir Everard Home lent, to permit a transcript to be made, some years since ? I merely wished to know whether I ought to present it as a Donation at the next Board of Curators, or report upon it if otherwise.

" I beg leave to acquaint you that the above-mentioned Volume is imperfect, containing only *Part the First* of Mr. Hunter's Introduction to a History of Fossils ; and that *there was* or *is* a *Second Part,* of about the same quantity of manuscript : and that this manuscript was one among the last that Mr. Hunter revised, and made large additions to, a short time previous to his death, is evident from the fact that a considerable part is in my own handwriting, with Mr. Hunter's subsequent corrections and additions.

" I remain, Sir,

" Yours very respectfully,

" WILLIAM CLIFT."

" *To Robert Keate, Esq.,*
&c. &c. &c."

The reception of the work is authenticated by the subjoined minute of the then Board of Curators of the College :—

Copy of Minute of Board of Curators, April 2, 1839.

"Mr. Clift laid before the Committee, presented for the Museum by Capt. Sir Everard Home, Baronet, the Manuscript of the first part of Mr. Hunter's Introduction to the Catalogue of his Collection of Extraneous Fossils, containing many of Mr. Hunter's corrections of the Manuscript."

The Introduction, as now printed, is a verbatim copy of the manuscript presented to the Board of Curators, the alterations having been strictly confined to the correction of mere clerical errors.

Considering this Introduction as not inferior in scientific value and interest to anything which has proceeded from the pen of the author, the Council have great pleasure in directing its separate publication, as an urgently necessary though long-delayed act of justice to the character and memory of him who founded their noble Museum. It is a new and astonishing evidence of his unrivalled excellence in original investigation and patient thought.

Scientific men had not observed and investigated with sufficient care and accuracy the organic remains of extinct animals and plants, their nature having been rather obscured than indicated by the appellation of Extraneous Fossils, when the attention of Mr. Hunter was drawn to them by receiving presents of specimens as contributions to his Museum. His sagacious mind immediately perceived the extent and importance of the subject ; he entered on its investigation with his wonted energy and indefatigable industry, aided by the thorough knowledge he had already acquired of the whole organized creation. He collected specimens from all quarters, ascertaining the localities in which they were found and the circumstances of their discovery, subjecting them to rigorous examination and comparison, directed by his intimate acquaintance with the laws of organized existence. He exerted the whole powers of his mind in long and repeated meditation, in the sanguine hope of discovering the nature and action of the forces which might explain the present state and position of the fossils. He thus anticipated by many years the views and conclusions of subsequent and still living inquirers, who have followed, with the advantages of more leisure and a constantly increasing accession of new facts and illustrations, in the path which he first opened. He had, however, perceived the true nature of these fossils as relics of animals no longer living on the surface of the earth, as having belonged to a former creation, so that, in his own phrase, they could not be " matched with the recent"; he felt that the extinction of such races, the imbedding and preservation in the earth of their more solid parts, the depth at which they are often found, and the successive strata overlying them, can only be explained by revolutions in the surface of the globe during periods of immense, but indefinite and uncertain duration. He may therefore be regarded as having laid the foundation of that interesting branch of science for which his modern successors have devised the name of Palæontology.

The attentive reader of the following pages cannot fail to observe that Mr. Hunter had made himself well acquainted with Geology and Mineralogy, according to the state of knowledge in those departments at the time of his labours. The inquiries connected with this publication have made known a circumstance nearly forgotten, but which ought to be rescued from oblivion, as throwing a new and striking light on the boundless range of investigation which had been undertaken by Mr. Hunter. There is only a slight printed record of the matter, which has, accordingly, been left nearly unnoticed by most of the biographers of this highly gifted man. Not content with inquiring into the entire series of organic existences, he extended his researches into the inorganic kingdom, and formed a large and valuable collection of minerals, which he was accustomed to use in his lectures to exemplify the distinction between the laws which regulate the growth of organic, and the increase of inorganic bodies. This collection had not yet been placed in the Museum; it remained at the time of his death in his private residence, and was sold with other effects, partly as having no connexion with the Museum, and partly to defray the current expenses of his family and of the Museum.

N.B. The word FOSSILS, of which the etymology is obvious, was formerly used indiscriminately to denote various objects dug out of the earth, and it therefore included minerals and metals, as well as organic remains. Mr. Hunter called the former NATURAL or NATIVE Fossils, as having been formed in the situations where they are now found. He designates as EXTRANEOUS Fossils the numerous and various organic structures found in the more or less solid external strata of the globe, from which they differ entirely in composition and nature, having become mixed up with their materials by the agency of external causes.—*Editor*.

OF EXTRANEOUS FOSSILS.

PART I.

EXTRANEOUS Fossils make one part of a class of preserved parts of Vegetables and Animals; and as most vegetables and many parts of a great variety of animals can either be preserved themselves, or make such impressions as mark the originals to be either vegetable or animal, which are lasting, we are at no loss to say what had been either vegetable or animal :—but for the understanding of which, it will be proper to take a general view of such preserved parts, and to give some of the principal leading facts to establish a principle respecting their preservation.

As vegetables are formed only on the land, and are stationary, and as animals are formed both on the land and in the sea, also inhabiting both; and may be said to be stationary respecting the elements in which they live; and as they are all found in a fossil state now in the earth which is not covered by water, as if all had been originally formed there, it naturally leads us into an investigation of the operations that must have taken place on the surface of this Globe; and which also, so far as the Extraneous Fossils go, leads to the formation of Native or Mineral Fossils. But it is to be understood that this investigation has nothing to do with the original formation of the earth itself; for that must have been prior to the formation of the Extraneous Fossil, which has only a connexion with the changes on the surface; therefore, as in the Fossils, our mode of reasoning on this subject may be termed retrograde; it is supposing from the state of the earth now, what must have taken place formerly; for we are obliged to take the facts, and guess at their cause; their history, prior to their discovery, being entirely unknown, and few relative circumstances leading to it, being almost left wholly to conjecture; for we have few intermediate circumstances leading from one to the other; the distance of time between cause and effect is too long for observation, and history gives us but little assistance, hardly a hint.

In this investigation we are obliged to search after the causes of operations from effects completely performed; but as these may be made out at some future period, their history becomes a kind of mark for future ages to judge by, and will be the means of correcting the errors we now naturally run into; all of which we should have been unable to consider, if we had not the preserved parts of sea-animals, each in a great degree explaining the other.

The Fossils of sea-animals inform us of the change of place in the waters, otherwise we could not have supposed it; just as we would trace the remains of former actions in any country by the monuments left, judging of past from the present.

As this is a subject connected with, or makes a part of, the Natural History of Vegetables and Animals, it has by me been occasionally one of my pursuits, with a view to match the fossil with the recent animal, and see how the present corresponded with the past; in which time I have, with the assistance of my friends, made a considerable collection*, and have arranged them according to a system agreeing with the recent.

Fossils are portions of the Globe distinguishable into their different species of matter, with their combinations, their arrangements, and attachments or mixtures, the Globe being a composition of them all. But for its changes, called decompositions and combinations, which are daily taking place, a fluid part was necessary, as also its vapours,

* The number of Hunterian Fossils in the collection amounted to 415.

the whole more or less combining, constituting what are called Native Fossils.

But it is to be supposed that any changes that may take place are superficial, respecting the size of the Globe itself; for we have no reason to suppose that the materials necessary to work a change are deep, such as water, and whatever it can take in solution, as also airs; for, without these two states of matter, no combination of matter can take place.

These changes are, forming solid matter into fluid, and from fluid into solid again; and it is in this last process that the recent vegetable and animal parts are, as it were, arrested or caught. But matter can become a solid without ever having been in solution : but water still had laid the cause of a separation of its parts ; and it was only a separation from this water that rendered it a solid, in which air gives no assistance, and in which operation both vegetable and animal can, and have been arrested. Such substances so caught, are either preserved themselves ; their impressions, which must be called a mould ; or their substitute, which is a cast : such are termed Extraneous Fossils ; therefore do not belong to the earth, as to formation, but having undergone a complete change from it of their apparent materials into substances which appear to make no part of the Globe ; and though in such a state, are not to be considered as constituting a part of the Globe, yet to which they again return to form again a part of it. And in this return they are discovered, many of which retain some of their form for many thousand centuries, which explains their origin, being only mixed with the matter of the Globe, or Native Fossils before mentioned. Some retain more of their properties than others, showing that both vegetables and parts of animals can be preserved when enclosed in the Native Fossils*.

* Fossils have been termed *extraneous* or *figured* fossils; but the term extraneous is the most applicable, as minerals are also figured; but they may with justice be said to be *extraneous*, respecting the earth, in which they are found.

As what are now Extraneous Fossils were a part of the system upon the surface of the earth, and arising out of it, but having now lost the power of the continuance of that separation, and are returning to it again, it is to be expected that they must be formed upon its surface, or at least at no great depth ; nor would it be expected from reasoning *à priori*, that we should find any preserved parts of marine animals, as it can only be on the surface of the earth not covered with water that they are now found.

But finding upon land more parts of marine than terrestrial animals preserved, and at considerable depth, it naturally leads to the idea of sea-animals at least having undergone this process at the bottom of the sea ; and if so, then as that in which they are found is now land, and as we find parts of land-animals and vegetables preserved nearly in the same manner, it leads us into a more extensive investigation of the permanency of the situation of the waters ; for as Extraneous Fossils are mostly found in the earth, or what may be, and are called, Native Fossils, it is proper to give some idea how the Native and Extraneous can be so connected as to become intermixed ; and in this inquiry we shall find that wherever an Extraneous Fossil is enclosed or imbedded, the surrounding native matrix was accumulated, disposed, or formed into that mass at the same time. And this leads us to the properties of the waters, with its motions, as also the air ; and to ascertain this the better, let us first see in what way they are now found, which will assist in some degree to discover in what manner they became so connected. As the Native Fossil which encloses the Extraneous was either so formed or accumulated at the same time, it shows that the superficial Native Fossils were formed in the sea, as it were, arresting the Extraneous ; therefore it might be supposed that the fossils of sea-animals, from their universality, should be found in every known substance ; because it is natural to suppose that as most substances have been formed at the bottom of the sea, that every kind would be formed there, but they are not ; for none have yet been found in granite. Probably no cause can be assigned for this, although several opinions have been formed, such as granite being the original matter prior to vegetable or animal; which may be probable, although we have no reason to suppose that the formation of granite is different from all others.

On the other hand it might be supposed, from the universality of sea-fossils, that it was only they that could be fossilized : but we find the bones of land-animals, as also wood, in this state; and many instances under very similar circumstances, though not in all.

We find the remains of sea-animals in every kind of substance excepting granite. We find wood, bones of sea-animals, bones of land-animals in free stone, gravel, clay, marl, loam, and peat. These are found, and at considerable depth, retaining most of their original composition ; and we find wood, bones of land-animals, as also shells of sea-animals, even in the same bed, encrusted; each of which I shall consider.

The vegetable and land-animal substance show that the sea has overflowed the land, and that it has afterwards left it, so as a second time to be land again ; for it is on what is now land that all those Fossils are found which must have been formerly covered with water; but previous to that it must have been land, which last is not absolutely necessary where only sea productions are found. The impression of the soft vegetable substance shows that the operation of laying countries under water has probably been quick, so as to overflow a whole country at once, and that the disposition of such matter as was capable of surrounding the vegetable matter which lay on the surface of the earth has taken place soon, viz. before their soft substance became rotten : and this could arise only from such matter being only mixed with the water arising from such agitation, which would be principally clay, and in such substances such Fossils are formed.

From the supposition of Fossils being formed at the bottom of waters, and principally of the sea, I think there are many circumstances attending their appearance which give strong hints relative to many interesting facts respecting the operations of this body of water; and several other circumstances respecting the changes of the matter composing the surface of the Globe itself, with their effects upon such parts of animals and vegetables as are preservable. They show the accretion, crystallization, precipitation, and subsiding of solid matter, or of all the different earths, both common and metallic, in all their different ways, which must have been either mixed or suspended in solution in the water prior to these formations we now find; they show the vast time the sea must have been, in some places, to give us such depths of new accreted matter.

Perhaps the depth in the earth of Extraneous Fossils might give us the quantity of depth of earth of Native Fossils, formed at any one time of the residence of the sea in the same place; as we are led to suppose that the bottom of waters are nearer to the centre of gravity than what the land is, more especially the bottom of the sea; that when the surface of the waters is nearer to this centre than the surface of dry land, and as the sea must have at some period overflowed the now land, gives us a hint of the variation that must have taken place in the centre of gravity of the earth, and also as the Fossils now found in countries whose climate does not correspond with the climates now inhabited by the recent (which implies that the Fossils can be matched by the recent), we are led to suppose there has been an alteration in the ecliptic; and they also give us a hint what vegetables and animals are probably lost, or are not now found. The first of these, viz. the Fossil, not being readily matched when fully settled, will in some degree explain the second.

Not only the formation, or rather the mode of preservation of wood and animals is shown by their intermixture with the native, but the formation of Native Fossils is also shown by the vast variety of parts of sea-animals being found encased in them, and of all kinds of earths, viz. calcareous earth, flint, crystals, clay, sand, metals, as we often find iron and the pyrites joined with the Extraneous Fossil, and in all states of those earths, viz. some in powder, as chalk; wet powder, as clay; others are crystallized, as flint, sand; calcareous earth, as marble, spar, &c.: but I have observed that we do not find Extraneous Fossils in granite, and yet we have no reason for supposing that the formation of granite is different from any of the others.

The great depth and quantity of those Extraneous Fossils shows that the sea must have been a considerable time there; however, the history of countries has shown this, without having recourse to collateral circumstances to prove it; for no Extraneous Fossils now found are within the period of history, not even those bones of land-animals found in peat, sand, gravel, clay, or those encrusted, which are most probably the most recent of all.

The change in the ecliptic would appear by the Fossils and recent of the same species having changed countries respecting warmth; for the Fossils of this and other cold countries are the most recent in the warm; yet this is not universally the case, for I believe that bones of the Elephant are found in all climates.

It is very common to find in this country, as also in North America*, bones of Elephants which are known by their teeth. It is the same with the Sea-horse, as also the Amphibia, as the Turtle, with many shells of warm climates, &c.; a thing that most probably would not have happened if a change in the situation of this Globe respecting the sun had not taken place; however, there are very few Fossils that can be matched with the recent, or that the recent are not known now to exist: yet though very few Fossils correspond with the recent, though very similar, yet they may not be of different species, but

---

* The large tusks found in America do not belong to the animal whose teeth we find. I have a grinder of an Elephant sent me from the same place.

varieties; for there is no more reason for an animal in the sea varying from its original, from a difference in soil and other circumstances, than there is for those upon land, which we see they do; but if they are really different species, then we must suppose the old are lost; therefore a new creation must have taken place.

But that many are actually lost is, I think, plainly shown, by the remains of land-animals that are now not known. Yet how they became extinct is not easily accounted for; for although we must suppose that the species of Deer to which belonged the bones and horns now found in the island of Great Britain, more particularly in Scotland, and still more in Ireland, is lost, yet we have reason to believe they were coeval with the Elephant; for I have the lower jaw and tooth of an Elephant that were dug up at Ougle [Oundle], in Northamptonshire, twelve feet below the surface, in a strong blue clay; and with it, one of the horns of the large Deer.

As most of the Extraneous Fossils we find are the remains of sea-animals, it becomes the basis of our argument that the superficial Native Fossils were formed or accumulated at the bottom of the waters, and therefore we must suppose that the sea must have been in those situations where we now find the Extraneous Fossils; and there they must have been fossilized while the sea was upon them. This leads to the investigation of what might be called the progressive motion of the waters; but how far there is any systematical regularity in this shifting of the sea, time alone can discover; for (abstracted from the reasoning upon these preserved parts of vegetables and animals) there are little signs of it.

We may observe that most countries have some of both vegetables and animals peculiar to themselves, although many vegetables and animals are common to every one; and this peculiarity is more confined to latitude than longitude; therefore if we were to reason entirely from the present vegetables and animals on this Globe, we should suppose that the vegetables and animals found in a fossil state in any latitude would correspond with the recent vegetable and animal of the same latitude; but we find this not to be universally the case in every vegetable or animal, although it is in some; therefore leads to a supposition that not only the sea had shifted its position respecting the surface of the Globe, but that the position of the poles respecting the sun had been altered, so as to have thrown different surfaces of the Globe opposite to the sun, which might be the cause of the waters shifting; and this supposition arises from the fossil parts of animals of one climate being found recent in that of another, instances of which we have many; and many recent animals of a peculiar climate are found in a fossil state universally, while many are not yet matched in any. I shall only take the Elephant as an instance of the second: I suppose that this animal can only live in a warm climate. The preserved bones of Elephants being almost universally found, is a proof of their having been either at one time, or at different periods, a very universal animal. Romé de L'Isle, in page 608, vol. ii. of his 'Crystallographie,' observes, that the bones of Elephants and other large quadrupeds are not only found near the rivers Ob, Jenisei, Lena, Mangazea, Trugon, &c. in Siberia, but also along the Mississippi and Ohio in America; and in our climates along the rivers Tiber, Thames, Rhine, Vistula, Elbe, Weser, La Lippe, Meuse, Moselle, Danube, Rhone, and the Seine; from which he infers that all these rivers are the remains of ancient currents by which the great inland waters have retired.

A Dutchman brought home a number of bones of some large animal from the Dutch Settlements in South America, which he supposed to be human. I had not an opportunity of comparing them with the Elephant. As the Elephant is an animal of a warm climate, it could not be universal at the same time; nor could it be universal respecting the Globe at different periods, if the Globe in every respect had continued the same; for if the Globe continued stationary, so must the Elephant. The same observations are applicable to the Rhinoceros.

History gives us no determined account of this change of the waters; but as the Sacred History mentions the whole surface of the earth having been deluged with water, the natural historians have laid hold of this, and have conceived that it would account for the whole. Forty days' water overflowing the dry land could not have brought such quantities of sea-productions on its surface; nor can we suppose thence, taking all possible circumstances into consideration, that it remained long on the whole surface of the earth; therefore there was no time for their being fossilized; they could only have been left, and exposed on the surface. But it would appear that the sea has more than once made its incursions on the same place; for the mixture of land- and sea-productions now found on the land is a proof of at least two changes having taken place. If the situation of those belonging both to the sea and land respecting each other, as also the materials each were most commonly found in, with the different strata over them, and the situation of each respecting the surface of the earth, were well investigated, we should be better able to form some general principles.

To ascertain how such parts of vegetables and animals become so situated as to be enclosed and preserved in Native Fossils, as gravel, clay, flint, chalk, &c., it is necessary first to observe what must have been the various operations that have gone on in the formation of Native Fossils, and are still going on, on the surface of the earth; for I have already observed that wherever we find Extraneous Fossils, the surrounding matrix was then so disposed at the same time. We are naturally led to water as the great agent in all these operations.

I shall first suppose water the great medium of union between every substance that it can suspend, both by mixture and solution; and where it cannot in all cases suspend in solution of itself, it is capable of uniting with such fluids as are: thus it is uniting with some acids and alkalies, both solvents of various earths; while other acids make some earth either ·more or less solvable, according to the quantity, as the aerial acid and the calcareous earth; and probably a neutral salt, composed of acid and alkali dissolved in water, may make a third.

Water is capable of different forms, by which it becomes universal. In one of its forms it is pure, leaving all its combinations, or whatever may be mechanically mixed; and is constantly moving from one form to that of another, by which means it is in constant circulation: first arising from the whole exterior surface of the Globe in vapour, which is the purest water, being in the best state for combination; then falling on the earth for all its future purposes, many of which may be said to be immediate, such as the nourishment of vegetables and animals; sinking into the earth, mixing with such of its materials as may render it a solvent; dissolving them, moving with them to the great reservoir, as also along with it whatever can be moved mechanically by such means: this is like the circulation of the blood in animals.

As water goes into the composition of everything that forms a regular body, it must be constantly changing from one to another, as those bodies are constantly changing, especially on the surface, which may keep up the equilibrium; but as it is a compound, it may of itself be decomposing and combining anew.

The motion of the waters is what we may consider as the regular system of the world; the sea the greater part, the lakes and rivers the lesser; each formed out of, and forming the other. The lakes and rivers, though not the greatest, yet not inconsiderable, when we take in the valleys and low countries that lead directly into the sea, having been formerly the seat of the sea, making at a certain period of the retreat of the water, which exposed first the higher grounds, the great inlets, and in many places, from the formation of the surface of the earth, retaining the water, forming lakes of various sizes, becoming a temporary deposit for the water as it flows from the now land, as also a permanent deposit of whatever these waters may rob the land of; for I do conceive there was, in the retreat of the waters, a regular gradation, that from the whole being first sea, that many of what are now valleys were first the great arms or inlets, then lakes, and afterwards dry ground; and that those lakes that now exist were much larger. For we may observe that the rivers that supply those lakes are carrying along whatever can be mixed with them, and with such rapidity as not to allow of a deposit till arrived at the lake; while on the other hand the water which runs out is clear, because it runs from the surface of the lake.

Water evaporating from the great mass, the Ocean, as also other moist surfaces, is in the most pure state, which fits it for combination, and then falling on the land in form of rain, &c., soaks into the ground towards the centre of the earth, impregnating itself with every soluble substance, rendering it capable of again uniting in solution with other materials of this Globe, which it finds in its passage, and which water is interrupted in this course towards the centre by such materials as will not allow it to soak further on; it is led off most commonly by some declining surface lower than the surface on which it fell, forming natural gutters and pipes, which are called springs. These springs most probably run in many instances across large tracts of land, even continents, or across the sea itself, for there are many springs higher than any adjacent land*. These springs in many places are directed to the surface of the earth on which they afterwards flow, which are joined by others in succession, still gravitating, as it were, along an

---

* Possibly the New River Head might serve as high land, as an epitome of those great objects, by way of illustration, considerably overcharged with water, and all the pipes as springs conducting the water underground, rising and falling according to circumstances, but falling in the whole.

inclined plane, which has its plane of inclination commonly decreasing, which is always becoming more so the nearer to the stagnated waters, by the deposit taking place, which situations were at first great arms or inlets of the sea between the rising grounds before mentioned, and which now constitute our large valleys, through which pass the rivers, but where, before, they only emptied themselves. By this means their course is rapid at the beginning, bringing with them whatever is moveable, being only mechanically mixed with the waters, and as they descend their rapidity decreases, and of course they spread wider, and begin to deposit the mixed materials, raising the bottom of the waters in such places; but on the two sides, as the water descends from the lateral heights, there will be a quicker motion of the waters, and less deposit, rather washing away what is left, making deep channels, so that the nearer to the lateral heights the surface will be in many places the most hollow, along which the future river may run.

From tides, opposite currents, &c., heights will be raised in those inlets of the sea; and if the sea should alter its situation, the water in such situations will be gradually contracted laterally, between the higher exposed grounds, into rivers; and in many places where there may be inequalities of depths in such arms of the sea, such may form a lake; for at the mouths of many rivers there are what are called "bars," which are in some, rock; in others, banks of sand: in such situations, if the sea subsides still more, the deep water above such bars will then become a lake; but when this does not happen, and the sea recedes entirely, what was an arm of the sea becomes now a valley, through which passes the river in various winding turns, according to the line of hollow ground, becoming more and more winding as the sides may be soft or hard*. Besides, as the surface is constantly uneven, whatever current there is, always making the turns more quick by its endeavouring to go in a straight line. We

* According to the Abbé Man.

see, on the contrary, when the descent continues steep to the sea, no such deposit is made, and no such valleys exist, rather cutting deep channels, and the ground often rising perpendicularly on each side.

Also upon the same principle of the sea leaving such places, the rivers are elongated into what was formerly sea; passing along what was bottom of the sea, but now low grounds, which must always be the case where the sea is leaving a country, and the uppermost strata of earth there is composed of the deposit; therefore such strata must be gone through before they can get at what was the bed of the sea, which may in many places be very deep. Darley Moor [Derbyshire] is first composed of a coarse sandy stone for 120 yards deep; then comes a black clay indurated, of the same depth; then comes a body of limestone the depth of 50 yards, in which was found the bones of a Crocodile*.

In such situations the deposit consists of materials that were hurried along, but ultimately carryingconsiderably of its materials into the Ocean itself, producing all along where a deposit can be allowed, considerable alterations at the bottom, which so far composes the surface of the earth; in such places, this will be in proportion to the size, the slow descent, and length of the course of the river, &c. All Holland and the Low Countries have probably been raised in this manner, and its exposure must have been completed by the sea leaving it. From situations being so flat, their rivers communicate in a vast number of places, their current not obliging them to take any one lead, and terminate in a vast number of mouths, as the Scheldt, the Rhine, and the Maese.

This must be more remarkable with the Ganges, which runs through an extent of 1500 miles, and shall only descend 20 feet in 60 miles; the Nile; the Mississippi, which runs above 2000 miles, and opens by a vast number of rivers, with many of the other vast rivers in America, which become the great deposit of the materials of the river brought

* *Vide* Toulmin, 'The Antiquity of the World,' 2nd edition, 1788, page 81.

from the land above. The Vale of Pisa appears to have been formed in this way*. Dr. Nott, of Bristol Hot Wells, says, " Torrents of rain and melted snow falling from the tops of mountains wear away their vegetation and soil; the larger masses of connecting stone in course of time are disjointed, and roll down into the valleys, which thus increase their elevation, as the mountains proportionally diminish : thus was the Plain of Pisa formed." Mountainous fragments rolling towards the Mediterranean and accumulating, displaced a portion of the sea and became ground; they moreover divided, and formed new beds for the Serchio and Arno, which, according to Strabo, once entered the sea by one common mouth.

The Red Sea will in time be only a flat valley, through which the rivers which empty themselves into it will run, terminating in the sea in one or more mouths, according to the surface at the bottom, which probably may form a country like Holland ; and in all probability the Red Sea and the Mediterranean were one piece of water, which would have made Africa an island ; and it is very probable the Mediterranean will be some day a lake, like the Caspian and the Black Sea.

Probably the whole flat tract of the River Thames, between its lateral hills, was an arm of the sea ; and as the German Ocean became shallower, it was gradually reduced to a river ; and the composition of this tract of land, for an immense depth, would show it a gravel, a sand, and a clay, with fossil shells in the clay 200 or 300 feet deep, all deposited when it was an arm of the sea, and above which are found the bones of land animals, where it has been shallow.

In Touraine, a province in France, upwards of 180 miles from the sea, a district of eighty square miles, eight feet below the surface, [is] a bed of shell-marl, chiefly of oysters, nearly to the depth of eighteen feet†.

* *Vide* Dr. Nott's Account of the Baths of Pisa, page 10.
† *Vide* Toulmin, p. 145.

The extensive flat tract of land in Portugal called Alentejo, shows evident signs upon its surface of having been covered by the sea. There is a vast extent of flat country going to Portalegra covered with loose gravel, appearing of considerable depth; and there are also considerable heights composed of such materials; but those composing heights are cemented together like plum-pudding stone, only the cement is not so strong, and which probably was the cause of their retaining this situation or form. But the most striking circumstance of the sea having once covered this tract, and afterwards having left it gradually, is the peculiar shape of the remains of those elevations of gravel; for it would appear that as the sea left their tops exposed, they were washed by the motion of the surface of the water, where this motion is greatest, and pebbles were washed off; and as the sea subsided, the lower part of such risings beyond the general surface or basis were longer washed by it than the top, consequently more of the gravel was washed away, till at last they became of a pyramidal figure, standing on their apex, some of which are entirely separated from the broad base at the apex on which they now stand, but which was a continuation of the same projecting part; and so small is this apex, that you could conceive you could move them; others again are still attached to the original base, whose height is the same with the flat country of which it makes a part; and what is a convincing proof of this is, that the basis of this inverted pyramid extends itself along the surface of the ground to a considerable extent, how deep I do not know; and all round, and on the flat surface of the base is strewed the gravel washed off the rising part which now forms the pyramids. If the sea was to leave the Isle of Wight, the Needles would exhibit something of this kind, only that the chalk is washed entirely away. Besides what are now valleys, having been the great deposit of rivers, the sea has considerable motion, called the tides, passing up those inlets, in some to a very considerable extent, overflowing the land, either carrying off with it for some considerable distance, or often allowing the materials brought down by the rapidity of the river to settle where the tide extends.

These tides likewise affect the shores of the land of every country; and as they are regular, the effects are pretty permanent, varying only according to the winds, which in many places have considerable effects, from being pretty constant, being direct against some shores, as, for instance, a south-westerly wind works away such shore; but it is possible that the opposite side, where there is a calm, it [the tide] is depositing its materials; but this keeps a kind of balance, and does not affect the general system of the sea filling up gradually at the bottom, although it must have a part. Also alterations on the shores are taking place from the sea having a regular direction of its course running on one side of its shore in some places, carrying into its mass the land, and losing on another, by depositing its materials there. So far these operations appear to have affected the visible land. But as the sea itself has regular motions, we can easily conceive that some regular effect is going on at its bottom, in disposing of the materials of the land which were carried into it, to be disposed of according to their natures; for I can easily suppose that a direction can be given by the motion of the waters to the formation of a mountain, as we see given to driven snow or sand by the winds.

Currents of winds will affect the motion of the sea considerably, more especially near land, and still more so between near lands; so that the depredations and deposits will upon the whole be in some degree regulated by these.

From this account it would appear that there is a kind of system going on; that the sea is the great reservoir of the materials of this Globe, and the rivers, tides, currents, &c. of the sea, the active parts, without which the world would be at rest. When we consider the consequence of all these operations, we may be better able to form an

d

opinion of the mode of new increase of matter in some places on the surface of this Globe, in which will be vegetable and animal productions, which will give some idea of Fossilization.

Besides which there are volcanic eruptions taking place, which break the surface of the earth considerably, probably destroying the old and forming new ;—possibly the Straits of Gibraltar were formed from such a cause ; the Straits between Dover and Calais ; the west end of the Isle of Wight, broken off from the chalk hills that run through Dorsetshire ;—as also raising up considerable extent of the surface of the earth which is already formed, either raising up mountains on its surface or islands ; when such arise in the sea, afterwards increasing their height by scattering inflamed matter from its bowels on the surface ; exposing substances rather than forming them ; leaving (we may suppose) vast caverns underneath, in which are again, probably, formed Native Fossils. This may answer some material purpose in the natural œconomy of the earth, but it does not appear so systematic —not so much a general principle.

From these general principles laid down, it appears to me that there may be three productions formed and accumulated from the foregoing causes, which point out three processes or operations. The first is the formation of rock, which may be composed of every known earth ; the second is gravel and sand, which are only moveable rock ; the third is clay, and probably chalk, which in all probability are deposits only.

The first, or rock, is, I conceive, formed at the bottom of the sea, stratum super stratum, and being connected with the whole, is immoveable, except from volcanic convulsions : this may be of every species of earth that can be in the state of solution in sea-water.

The second, or gravel and sand, is also formed in the sea ; but not being connected, they are moveable on each other, and probably are seldom to be found where formed ; and what was originally formed in the sea, but which is now land, is frequently carried by the water towards the sea again, but can seldom reach it, being deposited in the arms of the sea, forming afterwards the mouth of a river; and as the sea leaves the land, they are moved on each other, so as to be rounded. But this motion takes place more where the sea terminates at the land, where the motion of the water is most considerable; therefore, wherever we find gravel and sand near the surface of the earth, I should conclude that the sea had been there, and had left it gradually.

The third, or clay, being found in considerable masses, I conceive is not so much a production of the sea as a deposit from the land; and therefore, wherever there is clay, there have been inlets of the sea, at last terminating in a river that moved slowly on; and this is to be found more along the banks of rivers, as also at their mouths, even some way into the sea, beyond where the sand was deposited, than anywhere else.

Calcareous earth has certainly been in solution, afterwards forming limestone, marble, calcareous spar, selenites, &c.; but this earth, in form of chalk, would appear to be both a deposit and a precipitation; a deposit where it is met with, mixed with clay, &c.: but it does not appear to be a deposit from the waters by a subsiding of their motion, as was observed of clay, when it is found pretty pure, forming chalk hills, &c. It would rather appear to have taken place in the sea itself, forming hills, &c., more than the basis of valleys.

The substances which were in solution will be carried into the ocean, forming more the materials that compose mountains than the mixture of valleys; however, some of it may be precipitated in its passage, forming bodies in the deposit that have no connexion with them, probably cementing others. Of these two modes of conveying the materials of the land towards and into the sea, the one is mechanical, the other chemical. The mechanical substances being of different kind respecting solidity, are accordingly carried to very different distances. Gravel goes but a little way; sand a little further; clay and chalk still further; and if we were to trace the mould on from an inland country towards the sea, in the course of a river, we might find the following appearances—gravel; gravel and sand; sand and clay, forming loam; or sand and chalk, forming marl; and at last wholly clay, which will be carried more or less some way into the sea.

Collateral rivers or branches will render the deposit in the mouth of the river less confined to particular matter. Gravel may be connected together by what was in chemical solution, and form plum-pudding stone; the sand forming freestone. The cement will be of various kinds, such as metals, particularly the pyrites, Extraneous Fossils, &c. As a proof of this, may be cited the hills which accompany the Uralian chain of mountains on the western side. These hills are stratified horizontally, and are composed of pudding-stone, grit, and reddish marl; they degenerate at length into sandy deserts, which extend very far, and particularly in long bands parallel to the traces marked by the course of the rivers. The largest of these hills are those nearest to the primitive chain, and consist principally of pudding-stone and grit, which is for the greater part cupreous, and is what the Germans call "kupfer sandertz." This pudding-stone or grit in fact consists of larger or smaller grains cemented, and united by green and blue calx of copper, with some argill and calcareous earth.

By observing the nature of these hills, we may perceive that mechanical suspension and chemical solution have equally been employed, and that the suspended bodies have been deposited in proportion to their respective bulk; for the pebbles or large grains have subsided first, and in conjunction with the green cupreous cement have formed a species of pudding-stone; whilst the finer grains, with the same cement, have formed a cupreous grit; but the gradation is so imperceptible, that the fine-grained pudding-stone may be called a coarse grit, or the coarse grit a fine-grained pudding-(stone).

The pebbles and grains have, as we see, been suspended mechanically, have been rounded by attrition, and have been deposited sooner or later according to their bulk; but the copper most probably was in a state of chemical solution, which perhaps took place by reason of a pyritical decomposition; and indeed what renders it probable that the copper was dissolved in the vitriolic acid, is, that beyond the hills [which afford this immense quantity of pebbly and sandy copper ore] and towards the plain, a series of hills composed of marl are observed, which abound with gypsum as much as the former abound with copper; so that it appears that the pebbles and sand, which form the pudding-stone and the grit, were deposited when the agitation of the waters, or other cause which had kept them suspended, had ceased; and the copper was precipitated from its state of solution by a subsequent solution of a quantity of calcareous earth which precipitated the copper, and being united with the vitriolic acid, formed the gypsum, which is formed so abundant in the above-mentioned hills of marl.

The hills composed of the stratified grit are undoubtedly not of a very ancient formation, as they rest chiefly on a calcareous bed; they contain a remarkable quantity of trunks of trees and other vegetable bodies petrified, or sometimes mineralized by copper and iron; they also contain the bones of land-animals. The petrified wood is even found in the hills of sand in the plain.

In these deposits of sand and mud are found the bones of large animals, such as Elephants, Rhinoceroses, Buffaloes, &c.; and indeed these are found along the banks of almost all the rivers in Siberia, scattered here and there, sometimes in greater, sometimes in less numbers. The beds in which they are found are mixed with fish-bones, glossopetræ, wood loaded with ochre.

Clay, from being a compressible substance, will be compressed more or less, becoming hard as stone, also forming select masses. It may even have a disposition to form itself into nodules; and probably some circumstance may lead to it, as having an extraneous body in it, as part of a vegetable, round which it seems to accrete, assisted in this operation by what may be in solution in the water, also forming what is called the Ludus Helmontia. The second, or that which is combined or in solution, will, upon the whole, be carried most probably much further into the Ocean, and there will be decomposed : some will be precipitated in form of powder, which is probably the case with chalk ; and others crystallize, according to their nature, and form rocks, or large strata of stones, which may be horizontal, or incline according as there may be a regular gradual motion of the tides, or current in the sea at the bottom ; as we find drifts of snow or sand, on the land, directed by the wind. And even the trade-winds, by giving a regular motion to the waters, may assist in these operations.

These may form mountains and valleys ; or mountains may probably be formed, as has been supposed, by subterraneous heats raising water into steam*, heaving up large tracts of surface, but which would hardly form such length of ridges of mountains for many hundred miles with such regularity as we find them ; at least, the eruptions that now take place on the land do not produce such. Or whether the vast valleys are only so many parts sunk, which are equally explicable upon the appearance, but which are not to the present purpose. These substances will be of every possible earth, such as calcareous, argillaceous, siliceous, &c.; and according as one species of matter takes the lead, it there goes on, and there such will be predominant. Some will form pebbles or gravel, which will again be united either by hard or soft substances : from hence it would appear that the motion of the waters in all their modes, with the power of solution, appear to be the regulators of the formation of the surface of this globe.

From these observations it will appear that I consider the principle

* The Rev. Dr. Michel, F.R.S.

of the changes that take place on the surface of this earth depends upon the waters having earth of all kinds suspended in them, either mechanically or chemically, and separating from them either by simply subsiding; or the compound being decomposed, and then precipitated, as chalk; or crystallizing, forming rocks, and probably attracted by some substance on which they crystallize, forming what are called Native Fossils. In all these operations enclosing whatever substance may be in the way which may become a nucleus; as parts of animals, forming what are called Extraneous Fossils, which last may be considered as foreign to that upon which it is formed.

But we must see from this account, that in time the effect must destroy the cause; the bottom of the sea must in the end become nearly equal to the land; and that the waters, from the same mode of reasoning, should appear to be gaining upon the land in the same proportion; but this last does not appear to be the case, which would incline us to believe that the water was rather losing; therefore I must suppose there is some power or some principle, which will come in time into action to restore the necessary quantity of water, as also oblige the water to leave what is now sea, and flow upon that which is now land. There are strong marks even in this island, of the sea having left the land for some way, even since it has been inhabited: these are works of art, which have a relation to both sea and land; such as had been placed on the land for the purpose of securing vessels, which we must suppose were then near the edge of the water, but which are now too far distant from the water to be made use of.

A change in the centre of gravity of the earth might produce such effects, or some attractive external principle, producing what might be called a great and permanent tide.

In all of nature's operations we may observe that they always tend to destroy themselves. But there is, on the other hand, a restorative principle; it is like the hour-glass requiring being turned as soon as run down : but in the hour-glass we have not the principle of inversion arising out of the effect being completed, as we have in natural things ; and indeed, in whatever way the raising of the bottom of the sea is accounted for, we must ultimately suppose such a principle : for if the bottom is raised by any such power underneath, either by steam or volcanic eruptions, which arise from the same principle, a space somewhere must be formed, into which the water will rush ; and a repetition of them would bring the whole water towards the centre under the surface ; therefore, from such a principle, the waters would be gradually losing on the surface, and equally require a restorative principle.

These changes can only take place where the waters are in a fluid state ; for where it is constantly frozen, no decomposition nor combination can be formed, as at the poles ; therefore it must always remain sea, there can be no land : nor can an Extraneous Fossil form there ; for first, probably, there cannot be the materials ; and if they could be conveyed there by accident, they would be preserved in their original state, as was the case with the Rhinoceros found in the bank of the River Vilna, (Wilna) about 64° north latitude.

If the operations here described are constantly going on, we may plainly discern how everything that is preservable in itself may be mixed or involved, as we really find them : and as many Native Fossils are detached, carried along, and deposited at a distance from their [place of] formation, making heterogeneous masses, they may be called foreign or exotic.

It may be necessary upon the present occasion to give some general idea of what possibly can contribute towards an Extraneous Fossil ; viz. what it is in the vegetable that gives rise to a vegetable fossil ; as also what it is in the animal that gives rise to an animal fossil.

This will require a description of the nature of every thing called an Extraneous Fossil ; for no definition can be given that will suit every one, except simply that which strikes the eye, and which in a general way is pretty correct. For as Extraneous Fossils have been and can be matched by such substances in a recent state, and probably the animals most, they may in a general way be distinguished, and this arises from the part in a fossil state having been more or less deprived of the parts belonging to the recent, which is the animal part, and which is what principally gives colour to them : thus fossil shells have none of those bright colours found in the recent; yet some shells retain something of their original colour, although the animal part is dissolved into a kind of mucus, which would make us conceive that both the animal and earthy parts were so disposed as to reflect nearly the same colours, but the animal part is by much the brightest : for it is not simply the state in which the substance is that constitutes a fossil, but it is the state, with the mode in which it was brought to that state, that commonly constitutes a fossil; for many things might be called an Extraneous Fossil when considering it abstractedly from its manner of being brought to that state, for every churchyard would produce fossils.

Nor will mode alone give a full definition of a fossil, for we hardly term a thing a fossil that has all the properties of the original. We should hardly call a bone or shell, a fossil, which retained the animal part, because that animal part cannot be called fossil, for it is still in itself perishable. However, everything of animal that is found in the earth that is not more preservable than matter in common, may be called extraneous, and therefore respecting its situation it may be termed a fossil, being as much a part of the earth as any Extraneous Fossil whatever. But this cannot apply to a vegetable, for every part of a vegetable is perishable or changeable ; and if we suppose that wood is changed into coal, then coal is no more than fossil wood ; therefore a vegetable, as a vegetable, cannot be reckoned a fossil. But if we take in the manner of its being there, and if that should not agree with what we indisputably call a fossil, then Extraneous Fossil becomes more confined, taking in both its manner of production and its state.

The word "petrifaction" has served as a kind of definition; but I conceive it is erroneous in every explanation that can be given to it; for a thing petrified is a thing turned into stone: a natural idea, though not a just one, for I apprehend that no vegetable matter can be turned into a stone; the change of a vegetable for stone has led to this idea.

"Incrustation" is reckoned another mode of the formation of a fossil; but it is seldom we find things incrusted free from some of their original properties, either having the animal matter or the phosphoric acid, which the bones at Gibraltar still in some degree retain; and I conceive that incrustation leads to a peculiar mode of preservation of parts of animals and vegetables, which will be taken notice of hereafter.

To establish the principles of Fossils, I shall set it down first as a principle, that no animal substance can of itself constitute, or be turned into a fossil; it can only be changed for a fossil*. This is supposing that every change in animal matter is that of returning to its mother earth: but even here, if it could retain its form, it would be called a fossil; but if all animal matter was only to rot, and be changed into an earth, it would most probably be so small in quantity as not in the least to keep up the original form, even if it were to crystallize, or form itself into a solid mass of earth; but it has been discovered of late years that animal substance is convertible into oil, such as

---

* It may be proper here to explain this a little further. What I mean by animal substance, is every thing that constitutes animal matter which is not earth; and as bones and shells, both of them, have earth in their composition, they are capable of being rendered fossil: but wood has nothing but what is vegetable, therefore the whole is perishable; of consequence, wood, as wood, can never be reckoned fossil, not being endowed with the two properties constituting a fossil.

spermaceti. How far critics will consider such as a fossil I will not say.

Therefore, no vegetable matter, as vegetable, nor animal matter, as animal, ever can go into the composition of a fossil.

But we find vegetables preserved in the earth retaining their original properties; but such I believe are seldom called fossils : but we have many Extraneous Fossils imitating all the appearance of wood, many of which had wood for their base; we have also the impression of leaves, &c. But pure animal substance without any mixture of earth, stands still a less chance of becoming the basis of a fossil; for they are more dissolvable in themselves, or perishable, than most vegetables ; even less chance of having a mould formed upon them; therefore we have fewer of them. However, some animal substances are solid enough to preserve them a sufficient time to have a mould formed upon them, viz. the scales of the Turtle, Fish, and some Insects, &c. Even horns might be preserved a sufficient time ; however, of these two last there are very few in number that can have the opportunity of having a mould made upon them; but as we have no casts of the beaks of the Cuttle-fish in a fossil state, we may suppose that even this substance is not sufficiently preservable*.

The difference of the impressions of fish in marl schistus, and in the bituminous schistus, appears remarkable. In the marl schisti which contain impressions, such as those of Verona and Pappenheim, it is the skeleton of the fish which has made the principal impression, whilst the skin appears like a film (which certainly helps to make manifest the figure best), through which the impression of the bones are distinctly seen, as if the soft parts of the animal had decayed before the mould was made. On the contrary, in the bituminous schist, such as those of Eisleben, the figure of the fish appears complete, as if the impression was made before any part of the animal had suffered any alteration by putrefac-

* There is a cast very much like the cast of the two parts of such a beak.

tion ; it is probable that this difference has been occasioned by the property of bitumen in retarding or preventing putrefaction*. But many animals have parts composed of two substances : one, animal matter which is perishable in itself, as above described ; the other an earth, which earth, being the same as that which composes a part of the Globe, is not perishable, as matter ; although in some and so little it is perishable as matter, that it is supposed to compose a large portion of the Globe itself, being indebted to animals for it. Indeed many of our islands are no more than superstructure of coral.

Every part, before it can be rendered fossil of any one kind, must remain a sufficient time wherever placed, therefore must be such as will preserve their form a sufficient time for such a process to go on; it is from this necessary time that only certain substances can be fossilized ; viz. all such as are firm in texture, and more particularly such as have earth in them, as bones and shells; or are reducible to earth, and have a sufficient quantity of matter so as still to keep their form, as bones, hard woods, &c. From the great number of impressions or casts of vegetables, and those of the softish kind, such as Ferns, some Pines, &c., it would appear that the formation of such substances as become the mould were pretty quickly formed into a mould; because if this was not the case, it is most probable that they would be dissolved by putrefaction, as we find to be the case afterwards, for the vegetable is always gone and a cast in its place. That the cast is made immediately upon the formation of the mould in some cases, is pretty evident in some of the casts of the Pines : in some we find that in the centre or pith that there is a very different matter from that which constitutes the body of the cast, and appears like the pith of the vegetable. The only way to account for this is by supposing that the

* Since it has been discovered that animal substances when buried or immersed in water can be converted into oil, it may admit of dispute whether such oil is not a fossil; and if coal is a conversion of wood into such substance, then it may be disputed whether coal is a fossil or not.

pith of the plant really rotted first, and was immediately filled up with matter; and afterwards the body of the plant rotted, and the whole was filled up; but either with a different mass from that of the pith, or the same matter differently disposed or crystallized: however, it may be supposed that either vegetable or animal substances may be preserved for considerable time in sea-water, as there is such a quantity of water, and of a preserving nature, never of itself allowed to putrefy.

It may in this place be remarked, that such animal matter as is intermixed with earth, such as bones, is from this circumstance preserved much longer than if it had no earth intermixed with it; and we also find that the more earth there is, the less perishable the animal part is. Thus we have the middle or hardest parts of bones; also teeth have their animal parts preserved longer than in soft bones, or the soft ends of bones; and as a proof of this, we find that what is called "fossil ivory," found in Siberia, may be turned and worked as readily as that which is recent; the only difference is that it is rather yellower, owing to a stain they [the tusks] get from the earth in which they lay. But this may in some degree be owing to the coldness of the climate. Also I find in the fossil tooth of the Shark, that the bony part retains its usual part in form of a mucus, while the enamel part has its animal part retaining its structure and texture.

From this account we can easily guess what must be the parts of animals that are most commonly found in a fossil state, and what can only form a mould. It must be bones and shells, for nothing else can remain of an animal; and the moulds and casts can only be of such substances that are not immediately perishable.

The Extraneous Fossils we commonly meet with are what of themselves teach us all this; and as we have many Extraneous Fossils that are neither wood, bones, nor shells, although having a relation to them, it explains to us the difference between one fossil and another, all of which is explicable upon our first principle, of what can, and what cannot be rendered fossil.

From this we are led to divide Fossils at large into three kinds, but of which the vegetable only partakes of two. The first of the three kinds is probably the only one that can truly be called a fossil, which belongs entirely to the animal, and which are the earth of bones and the earth of the shells of fish (?), retaining their shape or form, although not their texture, as the Echinus, Encrinus, and Starfish; for it is their earth which is the only preservable substance belonging to an animal, and which I believe belongs entirely to the animal : and as a bone and shell have in their composition an earth, they admit of one variation more than the vegetable ; for wood found with all its properties cannot be termed a fossil. The substance called bone belongs to all the quadruped kind, as also birds and fish, both of the Ray kind, as the Shark ; as also fish in common, as the Cod, &c. ; likewise the Cuttle-fish : but in the bones of fish, more particularly the last mentioned, or fish in common, the earth is in small quantity, but most in the Shark ; therefore we find more fossil bones of the Shark than most other fish, and still more of the loose or detached ones, for detached ones are less likely to be preserved than those imbedded in stone, &c.; however, it is sufficient to keep its form when the animal part is gone. Shells, as far as I know, have commonly a greater proportion of earth ; and their not being united with the phosphoric acid, are therefore more ready to form into a perfect fossil state.

The second is a cast from the [be-]forementioned mould, formed of some solid substance, as stone of every kind, clays in all states, either in form of stone or slate, chalk, &c. The first part having been enclosed by such substance, afterwards the vegetable or animal part has been totally destroyed, forming a cavity in the surrounding parts, which is filled with the matter suspended in the surrounding water, or the surrounding matter in a soft state ; which cast retains its figure, so as to be known from whence it came or what it had assumed.

The third is the mould itself, often entire, at other times partly filled with various crystals; these two last are common to both the vegetable and bones and shells of animals, and we find that many animal substances have been so quickly enclosed as to make a mould.

When wood is found in the wood state, some of which is found in stone, it is simply preservation; but it would appear that wood, when long under ground, in some cases takes on the nature of charcoal. I have a stake of wood said to have been taken up from the embankment of the River Thames, the history of which is prior to any history of this country. I have seen it intermixed with Pyrites. From the preceding observations it is plain that a vegetable may remain for a sufficient time unaltered, so as to give a direction for other matter to be shifting the one for the other, as we find in most fossil woods, now become Agate, &c.; or where the enclosing substance of vegetable has only acted as a·substance to form a mould upon. This last mode I apprehend takes place only in vegetable or soft texture, which retain their form no longer than for a mould to be taken, and that mould to harden. Thus, then, what are called vegetable fossils are no more than either a change of matter, or a cast; and in leaves or soft vegetables there is nothing but the mould, the two sides of which are in contact, as if pressed together after the impression had been made and the vegetable destroyed.

From what has been already said, it must appear that the idea "fossil" has had as yet no fixed principle in itself; therefore, as long as this is the case, it must always be subject to dispute: one taking the nature of the substance called fossil for their guide; the other the mode of production or situation, neither of which will agree with every circumstance, therefore not with each other. As the earth of bones and shell are the principal part of an animal that can be preserved, and therefore rendered fossil, let us see if every bone called fossil is truly of this nature. I observed of wood, that we found it often with all the properties of wood. In the same manner, we find many bones of animals dug out of the earth, such as clay, gravel, moss [peat-moss], calcareous earth, as stalactites, forming incrustations, retaining in a considerable degree their original properties, but not, probably, in the same proportion with the wood; because the animal part of bone is much more preservable than wood, and will become less in every degree.

Bones have been found in moss in Ireland, in gravel in Scotland, retaining still some of their original matter, as will be explained when on the component parts of a fossil; such are often said to be calcined, which is an expression giving a wrong idea of the mode of fossilization, although both produce the same effect, viz. the destruction of the animal part; but how far they are to be considered as fossils I will not determine. But such do not come up to our definition of a fossil, probably in either sense, and therefore I have considered them by themselves; but if such are reckoned fossil, then it is the mode of production, or situation, not the substance, that is the rule; and every churchyard is therefore a bed of fossils.

Fossil shells and bones are found in one of two states: one, the original earth of the bone or shell, only the animal part decayed*, having all the original texture of the earthy part of the bone, &c., therefore not exactly similar to the above; this may be called the first mode of fossilization of bone and shells.

In many bones of this kind, we have the gradation towards the second class of fossils. We shall have the interstices in some degree filled with matter, and in many, these interstices shall be filled with the matter which enclosed them, especially if it should be clay or stone. I have a vertebra of a Whale that has been partly imbedded in clay

* It is not here meant the animal itself, but the animal part of the bone or shell.

which is indurated; but some of the cells have also clay in them, especially where a blood-vessel had passed; and, what is very curious, the internal clay is soft*, having been preserved from compression by the surrounding substance of the bone.

In some this is carried much further, where there is thrown in, or rather soaked into all the interstices or cells of the bone, where the animal matter occupied, matter of various kinds; filling these entirely up, so as for the whole to become a solid mass composed of bone; and this extraneous matter (or rather now should be called native matter), where a natural cavity in the bone has been pretty large, there it has crystallized on the sides of the cavity. This interstitial matter is commonly the same with the surrounding.

Another species of fossil is similar to the second in the vegetable; it is a gradual decomposition, and a new deposit; where the whole parts originally composing the bone have been removed, and an earth of some kind deposited in its place, keeping up all the same structure and arrangements as in the original bone. That this is the case must be evident, as there is not a simple grain of calcareous substance in the whole composition. These are commonly imbedded in stone, which mould shall be of very different materials from the cast, as in the vegetable. They are found single, or in such substances as are soon cleared of such, as gravel, &c.; but more commonly, I think, in stone and indurated clay: in these we have all the varieties that can possibly take place.

Shells may be said to undergo the same mode of fossilization, viz. the animal part destroyed; only, shells not being porous, there cannot be any new matter added; but in the cavity of the shell we have the same operation going on as in the larger cavities of bone.

* I have reason to believe that the earth of bone so far undergoes a change as to lose its phosphorus [phosphoric] acid; for when such is put into an acid, it effervesces as much as chalk.

We find the cavity formed by the two valves often filled with different earth; frequently very beautiful crystallization in it; the same in the univalves, and which is very common in the Nautilus and Cornu Ammonis, their cavities being not easily filled with gross matter. Some have, in the place of the shell, constantly a cast of a peculiar crystallization forming calcareous spar, such as the Echinus, the Encrinus, and probably all of the Star-fish kind, which would seem to have been decomposed, and a new mode of crystallization has taken place. Their structure in the fossil state is certainly not similar to the natural. It would appear that the original had hardly sufficient calcareous matter to form such crystallization, though probably not new matter. Such are often found in chalk, and filled with the same, or are imbedded, as also filled with siliceous matter from a pale to a black flint.

EXTRANEOUS FOSSILS.

PART II.

WHERE AND HOW FORMED.

THIS leads us in some degree into the Natural History of their formation, for it explains in what manner they came into such situations, with the mode of [their] being fossilized ; and we find in some degree a correspondence between the land- and sea-productions answering the short account of the alterations of the surface of the earth ; each will explain the other.

Extraneous Fossils, as they are the remains of either vegetables or animals that inhabited the surface of the earth, we must suppose, are formed either on its surface, or they are formed within it, but at no great depth. Those that are formed on its surface must have been covered with water ; which may be in various ways, and will admit of variety ; for some may be considered as intermediate, having been on the surface, and afterwards covered, either by the various earths deposited upon them, or [by] their sinking into it, or placed in large subterraneous caves, upon which water, impregnated with various earths, dropped. But I have already observed, how far we are to consider some of these as fossil, I would not determine; but the principal of those called fossil are certainly what constitute a true fossil.

This conducts us to bodies of water, but more particularly the sea, as the great fossilizer, being the greatest body of water. How far the lakes have the same property I will not say ; for it is asserted of Loch Neagh, in Ireland, that a piece of wood is changed for [into] a stone by being immersed in it.

As the sea has afforded the truest fossils, as also the greatest number, I shall begin with those peculiar to that situation. I have already observed that the rivers carry along with them matter of various kinds to the sea, and in two states, one mechanically mixed, the other in solution; and we shall find in the formation of Fossils that these two modes are employed in, or connected with the formation of many Extraneous Fossils, even making of themselves what is commonly called an Extraneous Fossil, such as either a mould or cast, or both.

Besides the sea having the fossilizing materials, it has the bodies to be fossilized. The sea gives life, and of course contains a much greater number of animals than what the same surface of the land does; for there must be such numbers as to furnish food for each other, which we may suppose is equal to both the land-animals and the vegetables. Such are constantly dying, and such parts of them as are not perishable in themselves, such as the earth of bones and shells, will, by losing the animal part, by time become what we may call a Fossil; and when they come to be exposed, or deprived of the sea, will be denominated a Fossil: and others, from being in water impregnated with such materials as are capable of imbedding their substance, or filling their cavities with such matter, will also be considered as fossil, for such have all the advantage that possibly can happen.

These have the materials of all kinds in vast quantity; however, some substances that are perishable in themselves retain their form so long as to be imbedded, forming a mould, which of itself is called an Extraneous Fossil. In this mould is often formed a cast when the perishable substance is gone, which is also reckoned an Extraneous Fossil. This would confine Extraneous Fossils to water-productions entirely, such as sea-animals; but as we have animals which inhabit both the land and the sea, perhaps many nearly equally, as [and] also land productions fossilized, such as wood, and bones of land-animals, it is to be considered in what manner they become fossil.

We may observe that the Amphibia, and such as inhabit both the sea and land, such as all of the Phoca tribe, White Bear, &c., likewise Sea-fowl, shall [will] partake of the before-mentioned mode of fossilization, by dying in the sea ; for wherever there has been a shore, there we shall find the Amphibia; as also many of the Fowl-tribe which feed in the water, called Sea-fowl, which may die in the sea near the shore, or be brought down in the rivers, will be carried into the sea, and be fossilized according to the fore-mentioned method, and will be found along with the sea productions. But they will also partake of the second situation, as in large valleys leading to the sea, which were formerly arms of the sea, or inlets [islets ?], which are to be considered as having been moving shores, as the sea gradually leaves the land, leaving materials it had robbed higher land of, raising the bottom, or forming a new surface, lessening the depth of water at these places, which renders it slower and slower in its motion, as before described, at last becoming a river. Such new land will bury in it such productions, whether of sea or land, but most of those common to both, as shall either die in it, or being brought into it, constituting chiefly such animals that inhabit both land and water, as also Amphibia, with land-animals that came there, or vegetables that were brought there, making a heterogeneous mixture. And I believe it may be observed in general, that the fossil bones of land-animals or birds are commonly found in such deposited materials, as gravel, sand, clay, &c. ; and I think, from the foregoing position of the accumulation of such matter, a good reason may be assigned for this. Gravel or sand is, I believe, always brought into heaps along the shore, probably seldom or never in the depth of the sea, although it may be formed there, and may be accumulated into different strata, both in the increase of the sea upon the land, or its leaving it, upon which will be placed many other substances, as clay, &c., which will be found on the subsiding of the sea.

g 2

But the preservation of vegetables and land-animals is most probably not confined to such situations alone. A change in the situation of the sea most probably has been a cause in the production of such Fossils, which constitutes a third situation of the production of Fossils. Therefore, to preserve vegetables, bones of land-animals, and many birds, one of two circumstances must have taken place : first, a change of the situation of the sea upon the land where such productions are; but in what may be called land-birds there will be a few of them ; for hardly any change in the land or sea can take place but what they can follow,—the new rising land, as it were, growing out of the waters, and abandoning the old, which now becomes covered with the waters. In such situations we are to expect Fossils of animals of all climates, as also vegetables ; and what would strengthen this opinion is the circumstance of two large teeth and the trunk [tusk ?] of an Elephant found in a lead-mine in Flintshire, forty-two yards below the surface of the earth*.

But we find wood in greater plenty fossilized, according to the first situation, than the bones of land-animals, and which was most probably in the depth of the sea; also wood which has been affected by the sea at two different periods : first, when in the state of wood it has been eat[en] by the Pholas [Teredo navalis?], and their canals have been filled with flint, &c. ; and then the wood itself has been changed, I suppose as above described. We also find wood eat[en] everywhere and in all directions by these worms, which we find eating the bottoms of ships at this day, and their canals filled with spar, and the woody texture changed. I have also wood whose mucilaginous parts have been destroyed or decayed, and the interstices, or first canals, which may be considered as sap-vessels, are filled with calcareous earth, making it hard and heavy; and when steeped in the muriatic acid, the wood comes out to appearance entire, but could have been crumbled down to

* *Vide* Toulmin, p. 93.

a powder. I have a piece of wood which has lost its mucilaginous part, and its two ends are as it were tipped with agate, as if half changed.

We find Fossil wood not much different from wainscot; and what makes me call it Fossil wood is, its ends, and some of their interstices, are filled with agate. The springs at Bath are often throwing up filbert-shells.

Also we find wood according to the second mode of fossilization, and in greater numbers by much than the bones of land-animals, probably in proportion as the quantity of wood bears to the bones of land-animals : however, I could conceive another reason, viz. that wood would find a much easier passage to the sea than bones, being carried down great rivers; and I am not certain if we have any bones of land-animals in the true state of fossilization, or according to the first situation. We find agate representing wood in every respect excepting in the species of matter : we find it imbedded in stone, as Portland stone, &c., and in such it has commonly undergone a complete change ; and what is very curious, it shall be imbedded in a kind of hard freestone, and yet itself shall be agate, therefore has probably undergone a change before it was imbedded : and probably the mode of decomposition and new combination led to this difference between wood and agate ; for as one particle of the vegetable is destroyed or removed, a particle of earth is deposited in its place, something similar to the double elective attraction, something similar to putting a piece of iron into a solution of blue vitriol; but the particles of earth deposited must be equal in size to the particles of vegetable removed, therefore much more in quantity than what there was of earth in the particles of vegetable ; and one could almost conceive that it was simply an exchange, for the centre of such Fossils are commonly much the hardest, while the outer parts appear hardly to be changed. This mode gives the appearance of the original structure of wood, giving the strata, as also the knots. Even colour would appear to arise from this exactness of disposition, for the layers are often of different colours, probably similar to the original wood. If so, then colour arises more from the mode of arrangement than from the kind of matter. But many of which Fossils I have my doubts of their having been [either] originally, or of the nature of wood or a gradual cast, for stone in its formation takes on strata.

But it is impossible to say what new forms wood may not go into; for when we see that the Bamboo can produce a siliceous earth while growing, which probably may be considered similar to animals while living forming calcareous [earth] in their excretions, as tartar on the teeth, the gout-stones, &c.; also animal substance, such as muscle, liver, &c., formed into oil after death, such as the muscle of a goose changed into spermaceti, it is not more surprising to see wood changed into an agate.

In one of the West India Islands, wood has been found either changed into, or for calcareous spar. At Frankenburg, in Hesse, grey copper-, or as it is called, grey silver-ore, is found in the form of a variety of vegetable bodies, such as wood, Pine cones, &c. Iron-ore resembling wood is found in mines on the river Jenissa in Siberia, and is called Sideroxyle.

True Fossil wood is not always found in stone or in the earth. It has been found on the surface of the highest grounds. Mr. Forsyth of Kensington Gardens has a transverse section of one [specimen] about a foot long, brought home by Captain Paterson*, who is now [1792] in New Holland, and gave me some account of them. But I got a more particular account from J. Thomson, Esq., of Chatham Deanery, Canterbury, who gave me two or three specimens of what he calls the Stone-tree, which he found lying upon the surface of the ground upon one of the highest hills adjoining to the village of Trevannelore, distant from Pondicherry sixteen miles. " The only observation I could make" [says he] "in particular was, that they all lay with the thick end to the north-

---

* Author of "A Narrative of Four Journeys into the country of the Hottentots and Caffraria, in the years 1777, 1778, and 1779."

west, and the small to the south-east, as if they have been thrown down by the north-west monsoons. There is no tree of any kind now growing upon the hill, which extends about half a mile in length and about a quarter in breadth, over the highest part of it. It has many shrubs growing on it, close about the trees lying down in their petrified state. I found one stump only that was perpendicular, and about two feet above the ground, the top of which had every appearance of having been broken off while in a stone state. This puzzled me, and I fully intended [to take] another journey and dig it up, and see if the roots were in the same state, but was prevented by my sailing the day after. I measured one tree lying on the ground thirty feet long, and three [in] diameter at the thick end. There were no branches on, of any kind, to be seen, except one small piece about two feet long and as big as my leg. In every part of them were perfect stone, so much so that I took great pains to look for pieces that might be credited to have been wood. I put a piece into a fire for three hours, to see if it would calcine, but it only flew when red hot like another flint. You will perceive they will strike fire."

As wood admits of having a mould formed upon it according to the second species of Fossil, [the wood] shall in time decay, and this cavity or mould shall be filled up with various kinds of matter, and this cast having impressions showing it is a cast from wood; but this has nothing of the strata of the wood, or knots running through it; [and] we often have the mould only. But this takes place oftener in Fern, the leaves of vegetables, as also in some that appear to be of the Pine kind.

The Amphibia, and the Sea Birds, also the natives of the sea, will be in many parts fossilized together, but not in every part, because they were, and can only be, inhabitants of the sea near to the shore; and therefore where the Amphibia abound, there probably was a shore or some large inlet of the sea, as the Mediterranean. However, some of the Amphibia go considerable lengths [distances] into the sea, and if such

die, the earth of their bones may be fossilized at great depths. Toulmin*
mentions the bones of a Crocodile found in Darley Moor [Derbyshire],
870 feet deep; the matter over them consisting first of sandy stone 360
feet deep; then a blackish indurated clay of the same depth; and under
that a body of limestone 150 feet deep, in which were found the bones of
the Crocodile; in which limestone most probably would be found the
shells of sea-animals. But those of the sea-animals will or may be more
universal, always where the sea has been; therefore the sea has always
been where the Fossils of sea-animals are; and which is most probably
in every part of the Globe; for in every known part they are found in
large quantities, and found in many places of great depths under
ground, which shows the sea has been long there. But the change in
the situation of the water covering land-animals and vegetable substances will at first produce Fossils of all kinds for some time, by
bringing with it fish, and probably shells; but few of those in comparison to fish, as they do not move themselves, therefore must be moved
by the motion of the water. Afterwards the fossilizing of the natives
of the sea will be continued alone as long as the sea remains there.

As the sea is principally the fossilizer of most vegetables and animals,
we must see the reason why the sea-animals are the most in number;
for probably those vegetables growing in the sea are not in any way
capable of being fossilized. The difference in number between the
remains of land- and sea-animals should be in proportion to the times
that the sea remains in the same place to that of its shifting, which
motion gives the only opportunity of forming the others, which difference is immense; as history has not yet produced the possibility of
the formation of a Fossil of either [a] vegetable or [a] land-animal. Thus
those that are constantly in the sea, as fish, but particularly Shell-fish,
whose bones [shells?] are more durable than even bones, and the
Cetaceous, ought to be the most common; the Amphibia the next,

* *Loco citato*, p. 81.

and the land-animals the fewest of all. If this is a just idea, then we should find Fossils of the different classes in this proportion; and I believe we do, which is a collateral proof that the Fossils are principally formed in the sea.

Where shells are found in chalk, marl, limestone, &c., it may be presumed that they produce the very materials that imbedded them; for it has been supposed that all calcareous earth was the production of animals; and, when considered in one view, it would almost appear probable. For, first, the earth of such is calcareous, and we find that in all calcareous earth, in whatever form, we always find most Fossils of sea-animals, and indeed seldom any without, most being a composition of such Fossils cemented together with calcareous earth, either crystallized, as marble, limestone; or in a form of freestone, as the Bath-stone; or between that and chalk, as the stone of Lisbon; or chalk itself.

Some blocks or masses of Cornu-Ammonis, with their shells, having been dug up in a clay-pit at Bath, I was desirous to know something relating to their situation, and for that purpose I wrote to Mr. Rack, Secretary to the Society of Agriculture at Bath, to give me as much information as he could, and he wrote me the following answer:—

"ESTEEMED FRIEND,—I purchased some time since some fine specimens of the small Cornua-Ammonis in masses, found in this county, and which thou mentioned in thine. The whole bed of them is now lost, and not a single specimen can be found of the same kind in the world. An account of the soil, strata, and situation of these unique Fossils I will trouble thee with.

"The place where they were discovered was a low, wet flat, about three miles north of a high ridge of hills; the soil a heavy brick-earth clay, in which not a single Fossil of any kind has been discovered, except a few Anomia at about a mile distance. In digging for marl about twenty yards from a small river, the labourers, at about eighteen feet depth, came to a rock of blue calcareous stone*, which, on breaking, was found to be full of these Cornua-Ammonis, of sizes from a quarter of an inch to three inches in diameter; but very few of them were more than an inch. This rock did not dip, but lay horizontally. On

---

* "The intermediate substance, as also the matter which filled the shells, was partly calcareous and partly blue clay."

opening the ground farther, they found it consisted of larger masses or blocks about four feet wide, two feet deep, and from seven to ten feet long, arranged one by the side of the other, in the manner represented in the enclosed rough drawing. The number was about

"The River.

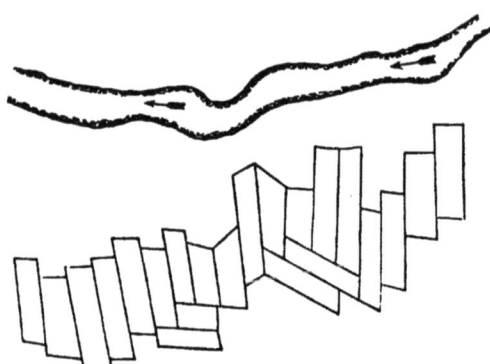

" Plan of the Bed of Horizonal Stones which contain the new Cornua-Ammonis with the whole pearly shell."

twenty; no other rock or stone of any kind was near them, nor a single loose Cornu-Ammonis found in the neighbourhood. The mode of their arrangement was very singular; and how such a vast mass of these animals should be collected in one spot without leaving a straggler behind, and become embodied in such regular masses of a stone quite different from any within several miles of the place, is truly wonderful.

"In general, the Fossil bones and Fossil sea-shells are found in the same, or at least similar strata. On digging for the foundations of the Crescent at Bath, Elephants' bones were found. And in the curious collection of the late Rev. Mr. Wickham, of Horslington, in this county, are some fine specimens of Fossil bones found in a stratum of indurated marl, and mixed with numbers of bivalve shells of the Helix, Cardium, Cochlea, and Pecten kind, with some Trochi, and multitudes of Anomia.

"But I have not met with any vegetable productions, except Fossil wood, among them.

"The leaves of plants, Rushes, Ferns, &c., are mostly found in the stratum called Wark, which lies immediately above our coals. Of the Ferns and Rushes I could send some fine specimens. "I am very respectfully thine, &c.,

"Bath, Nov. 6th, 1784." "EDMUND RACK."

This collection of Cornua-Ammonis in masses principally of calcareous earth so detached, is out of all principle or method, and looks like a Lusus Naturæ. However, this has been a subject much disputed; for although a great part of the calcareous earth is undoubtedly of animal origin, yet the same cannot be said of the whole; for without relying only on those calcareous mountains, and strata which do not exhibit traces of the Animal kingdom, and which by some are therefore to be considered of a more ancient date, we find that several of the elements of the granite contain a portion of calcareous earth as a constituent principle, schorl, felspar, and even quartz.

Now if we allow the granite to have been formed prior to the animal creation, we must also allow that calcareous earth has not entirely originated from decomposed animal substances, because we find this earth entering into the composition of several elements of the granite. This does not, however, in the least militate against what is mentioned in this part of the paper; on the contrary, it appears scarcely to be doubted that chalk, &c., which contains shells and the like, has itself originated from decomposition of similar productions.

FROM THE ABOVE ACCOUNT, HOW WE ARE TO EXPECT TO FIND FOSSILS OF THE VARIOUS KINDS.

As the Fossils of the sea, or water-animals, can now only be found upon land, it is a proof that the sea was once there, and from this alone we may presume that where the sea now is, it was once land. This leads to two modes of the exposition of the Earth: one, the sea leaving the land; and the other, the bottom of the sea rising up above the water by some convulsive motion of the earth at this part. I should be inclined to consider it in both views; probably great continents have been formed after the first mode, and islands after the second.

According to the first position we must suppose that where the sea now is, it was once land; if so, then there will probably be formed Fossils of land-animals which were then upon the land at the time, above which will be the Fossils of sea-animals as long as the sea continues in this situation. If this sea should change its position again, the bottom of which becomes land, then we should find Fossils of sea-animals and vegetables; and probably if this was well attended to, we might find it so. Therefore, wherever we find Fossils of vegetables and land-animals, it is a presumption the sea had come there, and then had left it, so that such mixture proves it to have been land twice.

This Island is a proof of this: we have in large blocks of stone, wood fossilized, viz. a cast; therefore the sea had invaded this land, at this time, and fossilized vegetables and bones of animals, then, its own productions, and then left it.

What number of thousands of years this would take, or how often this has happened, I will not pretend to say; but as the continuance of the water upon the surface is constantly fossilizing its own productions and can only fossilize the land-productions it finds, when it encroaches, the difference in quantity between the two must be very great. But this simply would produce more regularity of sea- and land-productions, alternately, than probably we find; and the gradual declining of the waters from the land, with the arms of the sea being the termination of large rivers bring[ing] land-productions into them, will imbed in its materials all of them promiscuously. In gravel or sand there are shells which are brought along with the gravel, and, as it were, make a part of it. But I apprehend that as stones are formed in the sea, and chalk precipitated there, the Fossils they inclose must be Marine.

I formerly observed that earthquakes* very probably raised islands; that on the surface of such there would be found shells, and in vast quantity, recent, dead, and fossilized; the whole of which, after a time, would be commonly called Fossils, and only because they were

* See p. xlv.

Sea-Productions, many of which not fossilized in the sea or by it, and now exposed by being raised above the water. This upraising of the bottom of the sea above the surface of the water, will also raise up along with it, all the shell-fish that lay on the surface at the bottom, as also dead shells, and in the substance of the earth all the deeper-seated substances imbedded or inclosed in stone, chalk, clay, &c.; which I have said constitutes the true Fossil. This appears to be the state of the case on and in the Island of Ascension; the whole surface of this island is covered with shells, and some so perfect as to have their ligaments still adhering. There is, besides, a vast quantity of lava, and other volcanic matter; all of which shows that it most probably arose in this way, because such recent alteration in the sea, so as to have exposed so much of its bottom, and so recently as to have the animal part of the shell still adhering; and the very name implies its rise. I suspect that many of those shells found on land near the surface, on the tops of mountains, have been exposed in this way. However, many, under similar circumstances, will be in the same predicament by the sea leaving the surface of its bottom.

There is another class of both vegetable and land-animal productions found in the earth, such as Oak, and the resinous part of Fir, found in bogs of peat. Bones of land-animals also in peat, in clay, in gravel, in marl, &c., which I conceive were never affected by the sea, so as to render them fossil from that cause, and which I conceive to be much more recent than the former. In peat, one could conceive that the trees had only to fall, and afterwards to sink down into it; but I believe no such wood grows in peat, therefore must have been brought there, and that only by water; or [had] grown there prior to the formation of peat. But the animals which could come there had only to die on the surface, and in time they would also sink deeper and deeper into it; and this I imagine might be the case with the Beavers in this country, whose bones are found in the peat mosses in Berkshire. Or, as peat is supposed to grow, we can conceive it rising higher and higher above such substance.

Bones are also found in gravel, clay, marl, loam, &c.; and as we have found the Sea-horse bones in gravel, &c. in this country, I am inclined to think that such situations have been shores or arms of the sea, at last constituting mouths of rivers, where the animals have been accidentally swept away by floods, accidentally drowned, &c., where gravel, clay, &c. have subsided, as before described; for it gives more the idea of being a consequence of the sea leaving the land than an effect produced by a continuance of the sea in the part, according to our idea of the formation of the true Fossil. But the difficulty is to apply this to the bones of some animals that do not now exist in the same countries where they are found; as also [to] the bones of animals that probably do not now exist in any country.

This looks like a destruction of the whole species of such animals at the time which [when those?] animals were probably confined to such countries; and which might also be the case with the Beaver in this country; and it being a more universal animal, its species is preserved in other parts. The same observations apply to the Sea-horse, as also [to] the Elephant. But many [of] the species being now extinct, either locally or universally, would make us conceive that the sea had made a quick inundation over such countries, and destroyed all the then living animals, and in a short time left it gradually again, so as to mix the bones of such animals [as] it found there with gravel, clay, &c., similar to those belonging to shores, arms of the sea, mouths of great rivers, &c. Thus we have in many parts of this Island the bones of unknown animals, such as a large species of Deer, as also the core of the horns, and bones of some very large animals of the Bull kind.

There are many more of such bones as are found in the peat in Ireland; many in Scotland, both in peat and other substances. I have, from the Duke of Athol, bones of the large Deer; as also, from the same place, the bones of a Horse; but the bones of the Horse are small, much the size of the present, or native Horse.

The bones of the Elephant are often found in this country, in clay, gravel, &c., ten, twelve, &c. feet under the surface of the earth; but I believe none in or under beds of stone. Toulmin* mentions the teeth and tusk of an Elephant found in a lead-mine in Flintshire, 42 yards or 126 feet under the surface. I have one-half of the lower jaw of an Elephant, in which is a grinder, found in solid clay, twelve feet under the surface, in Nottinghamshire. I have the grinder of an Elephant from the Ohio, in America, where are also found the tusks of the same; as also the bones [grinders?] of the Elephant from Siberia, called the Mamatowa Kost. They are found in the greatest plenty near the mouths of the rivers Ob, Jenissie, and Lena. They are brought to light by the rivers swelling and washing away the banks, exposing the bones, teeth, &c.

I also bring into this class the animal whose teeth are sent us from America, as also from Siberia, of an immense large size†. It is reasonable to suppose that this animal does not now exist anywhere. And as the Deer, whose bones we find in this country and in [a] similar way also, does not exist, we may suppose that the destruction of them both were similar; and as the Elephants, Sea-horses, Beavers, &c., do not exist in the countries where these bones are found, we may suppose that in such countries they were subject to the same fate; but such being more universal animals, the species are preserved where such cause did not take place.

* *Loco citato,* p. 93.

† As the tusks of the Elephant are found with, or near the same place with the Unknown Animal, it was natural enough to suppose they belonged to the same animal, and Dr. William Hunter was of this opinion; but as the grinder of the Elephant is found in the same place, that supposition becomes less probable; besides, the existence of such tusks requires the attendance of a number of other parts which the Elephant has, which do not appear in the bones of the head of this animal.

Various have been the opinions concerning these Fossil bones, which appear to have belonged to animals living in climates totally opposite to that of Siberia. From the observations of the celebrated Dr. Pallas, it is most probable that these must have been brought by some sudden and great inundation from the Southern to the Northern regions. In proof of this, it is remarked that the bones are commonly found separate, as if they had been scattered by the waves, covered by a stratum of mud, and generally intermixed with marine productions. The most remarkable specimen is the head of a Rhinoceros, which is preserved amongst many of the above-mentioned kind in the Collection of the Imperial Academy of Sciences at St. Petersburgh. The body of the animal was found, and was dug up entire, in the year 1771, near the banks of the Vilni, which falls into the River Lena, below Yakutsk, in latitude 64°. The skin and hair are still remaining.

The following account is copied from Mr. Coxe's translation of the extract from Dr. Pallas's ' Reise,' and which Mr. Coxe has inserted in his ' Travels into Russia,' &c. (*Vide* page 131, vol. ii. quarto edition.)

" This winter the hunters of Yakutsk found near the rivulet of Vilni the body of an unknown animal, the head and two hinder feet whereof were sent to Irkutsk, by Ivan Angunof, the Vayvode of Vilitsk. In the account of this discovery, dated the 17th of January, it appears that in December, about twenty-six miles above Vilitsk, the body of an animal was observed half buried in the sand, about a fathom from the water, and four fathom from a steep cliff. Being measured upon the spot, it was found to be seven feet seven inches in length, and in height about seven feet six inches. The hide was entire; the body appeared of its natural bulk, but in such a state that only the head and feet could be carried away; one of the latter was sent to Yakutsk, and the remainder to Irkutsk. Upon inspection, they seemed to have belonged to a full-grown Rhinoceros; and, as the head was entirely covered with the skin, there could be no doubt of the fact. On one side the small hairs were still perfect. The exterior organization was well preserved, and the eyelids were not entirely corrupted. Here and there under the skin, and the bones, and also in the hollow part of the skull, was found a slimy substance, the remains of the putrid flesh; and upon the feet, besides the slime, parts of the tendons and sinews were observed. Both the horn and the hoofs were wanting; but the hollow in which the horn had been set, and the edge of the skin which encircled its base being apparent, and the cloven separation of the hoofs being visible, afforded undoubted proof that the animal was a Rhinoceros.

"I shall here mention a few circumstances which I obtained from Angunof relative to the place where the remains of the Rhinoceros were discovered; and shall add a few conjectures upon the possibility of their preservation during so long period.

"The country about the Vilni is mountainous, and the mountains consist of strata partly of sand and limestone, and partly of clay mixed with many pebbles. The body was found in a hill composed of sand and pebbles, about fifteen fathoms high; it was buried deep in a coarse gravelly sand, and was preserved by the frost, as the ground in that part is never thawed at any considerable depth. The warmest and most exposed places are thawed about two ells deep by the sun; but the lower parts, which are formed of clay and sand, are, even at the end of summer, frozen at no more than half an ell below the surface. Without this circumstance it would have been impossible that the skin and other parts of this quadruped should have been preserved for so long a time: for we cannot assign the quick transportation of this animal from its native country in the south to these cold regions, to a later period, or to a less important cause, than to the Deluge; as the most ancient histories of mankind make no mention of any later revolution of this Globe which could with equal

i

probability have buried these remains of the Rhinoceros, as well as the bones of the Elephants, that are scattered throughout Siberia."

It is to be observed, that such seldom or ever have their interstices filled with the surrounding substance, excepting some of the larger cavities, which have large openings into them; so that whatever surrounds them was not in the state of solution at the time of being imbedded, while at the same time it shows that the soft surrounding parts, as also the marrow, was destroyed and the bones clean. It would also appear that they were recent in comparison to those of sea-animals, for they still retain their original properties, as will be described hereafter.

In all these we have not yet met with human bones; but in a letter from Sir James Hall of Scotland, along with a box containing some human bones, which letter I have annexed, there is an

" Account of a Hill in which Human Bones are found, near Rome.

" In a letter published in Sir William Hamilton's book, written to him by Mons. de Saussure of Geneva, a hill is described that lies about three miles from Rome, in the road to Loretto. It is about 300 or 400 yards beyond an old tower, called Torre del Quinto. A tomb, called Ovid's, is dug into it, and fifty or sixty yards nearer Rome is a gravel-pit, which is the spot in question. The hill terminates abruptly in a vertical crag, at the foot of which the road passes, leaving it on the left hand as one goes from Rome. This crag exhibits the internal structure of the mass, which consists of horizontal strata. The hill is about 100 feet high above the level of the plain along which it passes.

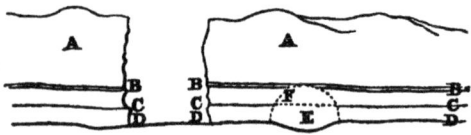

" 1st. The upper part, on which the vegetable earth rests, is a bed (A) sixty or eighty feet thick, of a kind of tufa or soft volcanic stone, full of lumps of black pumice of the size of a fist, more or less.

" 2nd. A stratum of rolled pebbles (B), of various kinds of stone, some calcareous, some flinty, and some pumice. In general they have undergone some action, which makes them crumble when taken out; in some places they are bound by a calcareous cement, and in others little attached and mixed with sand. This stratum is about three feet thick in one place, and tapers from right to left to the thickness of a few inches, on an extent of thirty or forty yards.

"3rd. Another stratum of tufa (C), of a different kind, more homogeneous than the first; it is of a dusky brown colour. This stratum is eight or ten feet thick.

"4th. A second stratum of gravel (D), with the stones lying as in the first, and composed of the same matters, though I could see no pumice here. The stones seem to have undergone a much more violent action than the first, as the greatest part of them fall to powder when exposed to the air. It can be hardly doubted that this has been the effect of the heat of the tufa above, especially as the decomposition takes place most in the upper part of the gravel. This stratum reaches down about twelve feet, which is seen by a gravel-pit dug in it, which goes lower than the level of the road, though not low enough to ascertain the thickness of this stratum, or to determine what lies below it. These two last strata join insensibly; for the lower part of the tufa has a quantity of pebbles, like those below, scattered in it.

"We found the bones contained in this box in the first stratum of gravel (B), between the two beds of tufa. We got up to this place by a bank formed by the crumbling of the hill above and the matters thrown out of the gravel-pit on the right side of it. There is the greatest reason to suppose that the place where they were found has never been moved since the tufa came there; that is, that the bones and the stones of the stratum were placed there by the same cause, and previous to the formation of the upper bed of tufa (A).

"The place in which we found the bones extends eight or nine feet from right to left, and probably goes further to the left in that place, where the stratum of gravel passes along the roof of the gravel-pit; but there it was inaccessible. We did not dig anywhere above three feet into the bank, being afraid of bringing down the rock above by undermining it. It appears certain that the bones were brought there along with the pebbles, loose, as bones, not in carcasses, for they lie scattered together without the least connexion; and their number is so great, compared to the space they occupy, that there would not have been room for so many bodies.

"Their nature is various, and indicates the presence of at least five or six distinct kinds of land-animals, and, amongst the rest, two individuals of the human species. The box likewise contains specimens of the different strata which form the hill; they run through it horizontally, as is seen in the sides and back part of it, where it slopes gently, and where they are seen cut obliquely, nearly in the same situation as here described, and in some places the pebbles are bound into a firm rock by a calcareous cement: this happens likewise in a small degree in the crag where we found the bones. I could find none of the bones bound in this manner, but sometimes lying below cakes formed thus. The last time we were at the spot, we found the bones most entire and in the greatest quantity; so that the mine is far from being exhausted.

"J. HALL."

"Rome, February 24, 1785."

i 2

That I might procure some more of these bones, especially those of other animals, I desired Dr. James Robertson, when he was at Rome, to go to this hill and examine it, giving him at the same time a copy of Sir James Hall's letter. In his letter to me, he corroborates Sir James's account of the different strata of the hill. He also took with him Mr. Byres, who had visited the hill with Sir James, but had never seen human bones, although he had seen bones of other animals. Dr. Robertson saw some of a very small animal. Indeed, it would be difficult for men not acquainted with the human skeleton to say what were, and what were not human; but Sir James meeting with a human lower jaw, which is most commonly known, [it] showed him at least there were human bones there. Dr. Robertson says that Mr. Byres never found bones there larger than those of Sheep, or some such animal.

This hill must have been formed before the Romans took possession of this place, and, probably, by the formation of the hill. The Tiber made its way in this direction, for it cuts the hill across. This is probably the only instance met with of human bones being in such a state. But in future ages, when the present rivers may take a new turn, [through localities] in which are deposited human bones, many may be found; for, in sinking the caissons for Blackfriars Bridge, a human skull was found twelve feet under the bed of the river; [and] there is in the British Museum a human skull taken out of the Tiber thickly incrusted with a brownish substance. Or when the sea shall leave its now situation, human bones may be found, as also everything of art, in a Fossil state; for, probably, prior to, or along with the fossilization of those we now find, there was no navigation. Indeed, in some degree that has now begun, for, near Ramsgate, a stone was dragged out of the sea in which was enclosed an iron cannon-ball; as also nails are dragged up incrusted with an iron cement, fixing to it shells, sand, pebbles, &c. But iron has the power of connecting detached substances together, forming something like plum-pudding-stone.

Parts of sea-animals as were capable of being preserved till fossilized, such as shells, must have often lain long at the bottom of the sea before the formation of the surrounding medium took place : this is plainly shown by the Pholas having eaten into them, which could not have been done but when [they were] lying at the bottom of the sea.

Many Fossil shells are covered with shells of another kind, but this may have taken place while the animal was alive in them ; as we often see the same thing in recent shells. But we often find that the shell has become a mould, and afterwards the shell has been dissolved, and only the cast left, and on this cast we shall find the shells of worms, and the holes of the Pholas, so that the cast lay at the bottom of the sea after the shell has been separated from it or destroyed.

Many shells are bruised, and have been afterwards filled with matter, which also showed that they have lain some time at the bottom of the sea, and that [a] heavy body or bodies have been formed, and put or fallen into motion.

Many have lain so long at the bottom of the sea as to have their cavities filled with matter, and afterwards to have the shell entirely destroyed, so that nothing but the cast remains, and upon this cast living shell-fish have fastened themselves, similar to their fixing upon any other stone in such [situation] ; all of which could never have been done if the whole had not lain at the bottom of the sea for a considerable time.

Many shells have lain at the bottom of the sea, where the water has been agitated so much as to make them roll upon one another, or other substances, by which they have been smooth[ed], and some of which have been afterwards inclosed in stone, &c.

Many shells would appear to have been lined with stone, and then the cavity filled up with sand. Many have been incased with stone and filled with the same, afterwards the shell has been destroyed, and left the cast in the stone almost loose.

Some shells [are] turned into chalk. It would appear in all of the Encrine kind, as also the Echinus, that after a mould had formed all around, and also in the Echinus, the shell filled up; that the shell had dissolved and crystallized again, and in a particular manner, for they break in flakes. This appears to be universally [the case] with all those substances.

The following letters, relating to the previous Memoir, are here appended:—

To John Hunter, Esq.

Dr. Caspar Wister's, jun., Account of the Large Bones found in America.

As you are inquisitive on the subject of the large bones found in America, it may be interesting to you to know that several bones, equal if not superior in size to those of the Ohio, have been found in several places of America. Colonel Matlark (Matlock) and myself have lately made an excursion to view the fragments of a large Os Femoris, which was found in Jersey, two miles from Philadelphia. It had been broken before it was known to be a bone; and from the fragments we concluded that it must have been four feet in length, at least.

Large teeth have also been found in the upper parts of New York; and at a place called Chemung, on the river Susquehannah, in the northern parts of Pennsylvania, a large bone was found in the branch of the river, which was supposed to be a horn, both by the Indians and Whites; it was sixteen feet long and several inches in diameter, but it broke soon after it was drawn from the water. I have had a very small fragment, and as it resembles decayed ivory, conclude that it was a tusk. The Indians say that the name Chemung arose from their finding a thing of the same kind in that place many years ago.

By the time our Society is ready to publish another volume, I hope to collect most of the facts relating to this subject, to publish in it. There are other facts relating to our Western country which are also interesting. An officer from there assured me that one of the fortifications (or squares inclosed by large banks of earth) could not be formed by 2000 men in six months. When we consider that there are many of them in that country, we cannot but believe that the former inhabitants were very different *from what the Indians* are now.

Letter from Major Rennel, F.R.S., to Mr. Hunter.

Dear Sir,

I have kept your manuscript longer than I ought to have done, but it was that I might read it over more than once, and leaving such intervals between the readings that the arrangements might in some measure appear new to me; a practice I follow with regard to my own compositions, for reasons that you no doubt have long ago thought of. I have been very much instructed and amused throughout, and shall be glad to see the remainder of it when completed.

I have indeed read it three times, by way of first reading, commitment, and report. As for the system, I cannot possibly devise a better: but the mountains I am afraid are yet too strong for us; since no system that I have yet examined will account for the regularity of chains of mountains, although we may easily form single ones, either by steam or by volcanic eruptions.

I am much pleased with your taking up the matter as it relates to the *changes of surface* merely; and not to the original formation of the Globe: and your suppositions relating to those changes appear very satisfactory to me.

If we compare the positions of the sea-coasts as they are represented to have been about twenty-one or twenty-two centuries ago with the present state, I see no reason to suppose that any great alterations have taken place, with the exception of the formation of some narrow slips of sandy and boggy land, made by the earth and sand washed down by the mountain torrents; and also to the additions made to the *deltas of rivers*: therefore, if the ocean is decreasing, it must be by very small degrees; and the date of the operations, described in your paper, must either have been going on at a rate scarce perceptible by the changes produced in twenty centuries, or must have suffered some sudden change after the process was carried on to a certain length.

This leads me to remark that, in page 3, you have used the term " many thousand centuries," which brings us almost to the *yogues* of the Hindoos. Now, although I have no quarrel with any opinions relating to the antiquity of the Globe, yet there are a description of persons, very numerous and very respectable in every point but their pardonable superstitions, who will dislike any mention of a specific period that ascends beyond 6000 years; I would therefore, with submission, qualify the expression by many thousand "YEARS" instead of "CENTURIES."

In p. 2, the term native fossils appears to be applied to vapour.

Page 13. The rivers in a flat soil (that is, in one of their own formation) change their mouths or form *deltas* by their filling up a part of their old channel by their own depositions, and then seeking a lower place; we hardly ever find that the two streams are comparable to each other in bulk or depth. This is particularly applicable to the tropical rivers, and which have periodical and very high floods.

Page 16. The account of the Pyramid (a very curious circumstance) is not clear to me, and may not be so to others. Some alteration in the expression seems wanting, or else an improvement in my comprehension.

If you wish to have any conversation with me on the subject, I shall be happy to meet you; but as your time is the most taken up, it will be for you to make the appointment, and I will let you know if I should be particularly engaged at the time you propose, which is improbable however. Please to name two days, and it will be very unlikely that I should be engaged on both.

Dear Sir,
Yours truly,
J. RENNELL.

Tuesday forenoon.
To J. Hunter.

THE END.